NAIL SCOUT

THE SECRET THIEF

ANNA MARGARET YOHAN

Copyright © 2017 Anna Margaret Yohan

All rights reserved.

ISBN: 9781973229148

DEDICATION

For my beloved parents and my best friends Kaylynn and Nadya

CONTENTS

Acknowledgments	i
One Evening	1
My Friend's Coming to My House	6
The Guard	11
My Thought	17
Auntie!	21
The Matador Bird	25
The Island	32
Where Was The Drasa Family?	36
Mystery Solved	40
The Snoring Agent	43

ACKNOWLEDGMENTS

I would like to thank all who enjoy reading my stories.

ONE EVENING

Do you know who I am? I am Nail Scout and every afternoon, I walk in the Wingfall Town Park, resting from the detective work, or thinking about the mystery I hadn't solved.

Yes! I am a detective! I am a

general of the Scout too. Wingfall Town was a small town (more like a village). The houses were the trees that had a hole to get in.

Detective and Scout souls were mixed very good. It's hard to be a detective in the Wingfall Town. There were many thieves. Being a Peregrine Falcon was great for the work chasing thieves, for Peregrine Falcon is the fastest animal in the world.

I went home, and read my first diary of 12 diaries included my new one. When I read it, my telephone on the table beside the fireplace rang. I hurried down from the second floor of my tree hole and went to the fireplace at the first floor and picked up the receiver.

I screeched, *"Hello? This is Nail Scout, the detective. Any help?"*.

A female Peregrine Falcon's voice shrieked and screeched in panic until my Scout uniform blown by the voice with my feathers from up to down blown too,

"Help! Ms. Scout! Someone stole all

my stuffs at my home! Help!"

I answered quickly, *"Just don't get panic! What's the clue? Any clues?"*, I asked calmly.

She said the clues were a blue feather and a long tail-feather.

"Long tail-feather? Hello?"

I spoke, but the telephone was closed. Long tail-feather…it's sounded very familiar to me. I couldn't remember what it was.

The voice in the telephone was Miss Joley's sound. I couldn't sleep for the night. I couldn't stop my mind about the thief. It's the most powerful mystery, why Miss Joley closed the telephone before I answered?

I confused and needed help.

MY FRIEND'S COMING TO MY HOUSE

The next morning, my detective friend came to my house and we discussed the thief in a very long time. My friend said that this morning, he looked at Miss Joley's house and found another clue, a typical claw that was like Garaga's claw, the most powerful thief in the Wingfall Town.

The claw's shape was like a knife. I kept wondering, was it Garaga's claw? Where was his house? My friend said that he didn't know what the address of Miss Joley's house was because the name of the street was scratched. Miss Joley had many guards at her home, and a bull for the security that she could order the bull to attack.

I was suspicious with one of her guards looked like Garaga with glasses. Molly meat! I was confused! The newspapers also wrote about this story. I tried to read jokes, but it couldn't help to forget all about the thief. I was very drowsy on days because I hadn't slept for days.

I was writing in my diary, when suddenly, my friend came to my house again. He flew in to my tree hole house and gave me another clue…a map! Molly pigeon! The map was scratched all the way, like scratched by a knife! There was an island…a new island that I had never seen!

Come on Nail, I know you can see the island's name! Yep! The island's name is scratched, I can't see it!.

I flew quickly to the island…with the map…but I was kicked by a great shoe back to the Wingfall Town. I sighed.

I went back to my tree hole and I called Miss Joley again with my telephone, *"Hello Miss Joley? It's me, Nail Scout. I want to ask you something…do you have a suspicion to a guard or to the other Falcon?"*

"Yea…I am suspicious with a guard with glasses. He always wants to guard my furniture."

Molly rabbit. I was suspicious with that guard too! This mystery made me confused and drowsy and of course, tired a lot. Why, why, why? Why there was a thief again?

THE GUARD

I closed my telephone, and I flew circling the town slowly. I saw something. A Peregrine Falcon was flying quickly. He looked suspicious.

I followed him. He went to an island…but he disappeared! The island was the same new island in the map. I taught I saw him with a guard uniform.

I went to the island and stood on a tree. The alarm system didn't ring. I was so grateful. I waited him to go out. He went out five minutes later!

He saw me and screeched, "*What are you doing? Get out!*"

I got out from the island quickly, but I bumped a tree and went head butted the guard's head. The guard fell and I was still on the guard's body. His glasses fell from his face, but he quickly took the glasses. Molly rats! I quickly flew to the Wingfall Town and went in to my house. I pulled my secret steel gate and I sat down in front of my fireplace.

My heart was pounding very fast that my heart felt wanting to jump! I flew in my home to make myself calm down. I forgot that I was flying in a super speed and bumped all of my house.

I sat down again, and tried to call Miss Joley again.

"Miss Joley? I hope you want to tell me another secret about the guard", I screeched.

She answered, *"Well, Ms. Scout. I received a mail that this new guard would come to my house one week ago. He told me that he wanted to guard only the furniture in my house. My house is empty now. I am so sad"*, she said.

"What is the address your house, Miss Joley?", I asked.

She said that it's on the White

Snow 13. I closed my receiver. I thought, that house was the Drasa family's house! How could Miss Joley come and worst, live in the Drasa family's house? I was really confused about this case.

Where was the Drasa family? Did Miss Joley want to ashame me? Miss Joley was my enemy. She became good to me from the day her priceless furniture and all the furniture in her house stolen. I meant the Drasa family's furniture.

My stomach started pounding. I

was really confused about this of course. Molly blue!

MY THOUGHT

I didn't really know what happened. I went to the Drasa family's house and fortunately, Miss Joley wasn't there. I popped my eyes to see another clue. Wait! I saw something glinting in front of the sofa! A priceless hat that belonged to Mick! One of the Drasa family's chick! The Drasa family had 3 chicks. Woosh!, heard a sound of the flapping wings of a Peregrine Falcon.

"Oh no…Miss Joley is back!"

I quickly went back to my tree hole house. I pulled my steel gate again and started thinking. Something strange. I didn't know…but my Scout instinct said that Miss Joley envied me and wanted to embarrass me. How evil! Holey great priceless golden eagle! I went out from my house and tried to speak with the suspicious guard.

When the guard saw me, he screeched, *"Hey you! Again?! Shoo! Or fight me naturally!"*, he screeched. *"I…I…will…will…g…g…go ba…back"*, I stammered.

"Too late", he screeched softly and PULLED MY FEET!

I somersaulted in the air after he threw me to the sky. I tried to fly, but I couldn't! I screeched and suddenly, wind-blown me to the guard's face and I hit the guard on his head! I went home after he was fainted because of me, and I had a taught, this guard and Miss Joley worked together to…what? Embarrass me? Huh?

AUNTIE!

The next day, I heard someone screeching. I was hurried going to the hole of my tree and looked.

"*Are you fine, aunty?*", asked a teen male Peregrine Falcon.

Yep! It's my nephew, the chick from my little sister, Sally. My nephew's name was Sonny and he was twelve years old, while I was 28 years old that year. Sonny always wore his taekwondo uniform with the red belt, he never changed to black (he was a senior of taekwondo).

"Hey Sonny, why do you come here, to live with me?", I asked.

"No aunty, my mom and dad were going for something emergency for 1 year! I'm so sad and I know I can't live alone.

So, I go to your house", he answered sadly while I let him in.

Magnificent! Of course, I had two beds and he could be a detective with me too!

"Just live with me and maybe, you can be a little detective with me too...", I screeched.

He said with his eyes lit up, *"Of course I've read the newspaper and I'm ready to help you!"*.

Did I mention to you that he was the nicest Falcon I've ever seen? He really loved books like me and I had a lot of books in my home for us to read.

"Well, Sonny, here's the clue, the first one is from your left side", I said while my wings showed him the clues, the long tail-feather, the map, and the other clues. Sonny looked at the clues very close until his beak touched the clues.

THE MATADOR BIRD

We had a plan to get in to Drasa family's house again to see the bad guard or Miss Joley or both the next morning. So, the next morning, we went to the house and saw the bull was sleeping. Thanks bird. I heard there was the sound of Garaga and Miss Joley laughing.

"Hahaahaa! I told you that working with me is fun…helping me to embarrass your top 1 enemy and the one to whom I always envy. Great job, Garaga! Hahahaa!", Sonny and I heard the sound.

Did I forget to tell you? No? Sonny was a senior of the taekwondo. He looked very angry and tried fight them, but I held his tail and he looked know what my plan was, to attack them if they were out. Just then, Garaga, the fake guard, who had just opened his fake glasses, saw me and shrieked to the bull beneath the tree,

"Holrey! Kill the falcon who wears a Scout uniform!", and the bull named Holrey woke up and kicked me by his horns to the air.

"Hiyyaaaaaa!", my nephew, Sonny, screeched very loudly. He jumped high, and landed with one of his hand on the ground in front of Holrey.

Sonny kicked the bull. The bull kicked Sonny to the air. Sonny clawed the bull until wounded, and the bull was face to face with him after Holrey made Sonny flat on the ground. I knew I had to take action, so, I split myself to a banana and landed square on Holrey's head with my feet!

"*Auntie! You are great!*", Sonny screeched.

Then, I saw something that made Holrey didn't focus on me, Sonny had a red taekwondo material on his waist!

"Hand your material to me", I ordered him.

He opened his material and I screeched to the bull, *"Hey hey hey! Yooho! Red!"*, and the bull became fresh again, and ran towards the red material.

I flew far and threw the material to the place I stopped and the bull was now only focusing to the red material.

"Sorry, Sonny. I will buy a new black material for you when the mystery is

solved", I said to Sonny.

Sonny looked just fine. We went in and saw that Garaga and Miss Joley were furious because Holrey now didn't want to do what they ordered. Holrey became wild again and went running to the far far land.

Sonny said bravely, "*Tell us where is your island!*"

What a brave nephew! Garaga, who had learned taekwondo falcon, but not a senior, fought Sonny.

Miss Joley screeched to Garaga,

"*No! Sonny is a senior, you waterbrain!*", but it's too late.

Garaga didn't win the small taekwondo match. Instead, he bumped to the floor.

At last, Garaga said, "*Ok, then, I will show you the island together with Miss Joley*".

Miss Joley mouthed to say no, but she couldn't.

THE ISLAND

I followed Sonny, who led me to the island and Sonny followed Miss Joley and Garaga to the island on the map. We arrived 5 minutes later, and got in to the hideout of Garaga's. Molly pigeon! The hideout of Garaga was full of the stuffs he stole from the last, last, mystery. I came to the police office while Sonny guarded Garaga and Miss Joley.

Wow, wow, wow. The first mystery I solved! (Of course, because I was a new detective). 10 minutes later, the police were coming to Garaga's hideout after I went to the police office and gave them the map.

I asked to Miss Joley after she would go to the prison with

Garaga, *"So, you envy with me because I am a detective, Right? I am agent YYY. And she succeeded to prison as the greatest thief in the Wingfall Town."*

Miss Joley looked sad, and there they went, to the prison. *"Thank you for solving the mystery, agent YYY."*

"We appreciate your work", said a policeman.

"Thank Sonny, my nephew, too, because he helped me solving this incomplete mystery", I answered.

The policeman looked confused about what I said, the incomplete mystery. The last question was, where was the Drasa family?

WHERE WAS THE DRASA FAMILY?

I spent the day with questions from the newspapers and TV. I still answered that this mystery was incomplete and what was incomplete. The Drasa family had gone! I examined the Drasa family's house again with Sonny and found 5 large chests shaking and thudding by themselves. Sonny found the key on the table. We unlocked them all and saw, the Drasa family were there, locked in 5 large chests by Garaga and Miss Joley.

"Miss Scout and Mr Scout! Thanks bird you found us!", said Clara, the mother of the chicks of the Drasa family.

"We've been locked for 1 week here or

more, and we're hungry now", said Mike.

"Oh, Mike, I screeched, here's your hat". And I gave them foods.

Mike looked very happy. Just then, trucks that contained the furniture of the Drasa family's house were coming, and the house became merry again.

"Thank you, Scout family", said the Drasa family.

The other trucks were coming to hand the lost furniture to the people who had them. The journalists started asking me and the Drasa family what had happened.

MYSTERY SOLVED

The secret thief was solved, and I could rest again with Sonny reading the books. His parents were still on the emergency things far away from the Wingfall town. Cards from all people to thank me kept arriving at my house, and now, the cards were more than 100! I went to the taekwondo shop and bought Sonny a new black taekwondo belt so no bulls would attack.

I liked this life and one very important thing, Don't give up with any excuses. Try to reach the sky. If you fail, just try it again.

THE END

Farewell, till' the next adventure!

THE SNORING AGENT

Who knew when one day, a new agent accepted at my detective office? What was his attitude, and how he did it? Did he like to eat? Watched the TV? Yogas? Rough?

Tough? Weak?

Find these great questions in the Nail Scout-The Snoring Agent book! Completed with funny objects and unbelievable actions!

© 2017 Anna Margaret Yohan

Terms and Conditions:

The purchaser of this book (paperback or ebook) is subject to the condition that he/she shall in no way resell it, nor any part of it, nor make copies of it to distribute freely.

All Persons Fictitious Disclaimer:

This book is a work of fiction. Any similarity between the characters and situations within its pages and places or persons, living or dead, is unintentional and co-incidental

ABOUT THE AUTHOR

Anna Margaret Yohan is a young writer from Jakarta, Indonesia. Born in 2008, Anna started to write books since age 9. She loves writing detective, mystery, and adventure stories. Famous authors such as J. K. Rowling and Elisabetta Dami have been her inspiration in writing books. She enjoys reading fiction and nonfiction books.